This igloo book belongs to:

....

Contents

igloobooks

Published in 2018
by Igloo Books Ltd, Cottage Farm, Sywell, NN6 0BJ
www.igloobooks.com

Copyright © 2017 Igloo Books Ltd

Written by Gemma Barder
Illustrated by Marc Mones

Designed by Amy Bradford
Edited by Natalia Boileau

WKT001 0818
2 4 6 8 10 9 7 5 3
ISBN 978-1-78670-673-7

Printed and manufactured in China

5 Minute Tales

Christmas Stories

igloobooks

A Christmas Wish

Mia wanted to write a letter to Santa, but every time she started to write, her little sister Lily would **burst** into the room.

All Lily ever wanted to do was play with Mia's best doll.

With a sigh, Mia took her doll and writing set downstairs to finish her letter, but Lily still wanted to play. She took the doll and had a tea party on the floor.

Sighing, Mia went up to her bedroom, but Lily was close behind.

When Mia wasn't looking, Lily styled the doll's hair using all of Mia's prettiest hair clips.

If only Lily had her own doll to play with,

thought Mia, feeling frustrated.

Just then, she had a **brilliant** idea.

Mia finally found a quiet spot to write her letter. She jotted down what she truly wanted, then placed the letter on the mantelpiece, ready to be posted.

She was so **excited,** she didn't even notice Lily had taken her doll again.

The next morning, Mia ran to the mantelpiece, but her letter had **vanished.**
"**Without the letter, I might not get my Christmas wish!**" she cried

"**Perhaps it flew up
the chimney to Santa?**"
wondered Mum.

On Christmas morning, Mia and Lily opened their presents excitedly. But Mia still hadn't found the one special thing she had asked Santa for.

There's one present left under the tree, maybe that's it?

said Mum.

Mia reached under the tree and pulled out a brightly wrapped present.

It's for Lily!

she said, excited

She passed the present to her sister
and watched as she **tore** off the ribbon.

It was a new doll, just for Lily.
Lily hugged it tightly.

My Christmas wish came true! said Mia.

"I wished for a new doll
for Lily, so now we can
both play together."

Clumsy Alf

Alf was the **clumsiest** elf in the North Pole. Each day, he sat in the workshop and tried his best to make amazing toys for Santa to deliver...

... but somehow, he always got it wrong.

It was Christmas Eve and Alf was determined he was going to be the best elf in the workshop.

He was going to make the **fluffiest** teddies, the **toughest** dinosaurs and the **whizziest** scooters.

Alf headed to the workshop to assemble the world's speediest super-scooters, but he didn't see a spare wheel on the floor.

Whoosh!

Alf **slipped** and **slid** across the workshop
floor and landed in a huge pile of teddy-bear stuffing!

Ohh!

cried Alf, as stuffing flew
through the air like a snowstorm.

"What have you done, Alf?" cried the chief elf. "All this fluff has ruined the paint on the doll's houses!"

The chief elf told Alf to go and clear the snow outside the sleigh barn, ready for Santa's take-off. Alf was feeling very sorry for himself. He just wanted to help Santa as much as all the other elves.

When Alf finished clearing the snow, he sneaked into the barn to see the reindeers. Suddenly, he heard loud footsteps. It was Santa and the chief elf!

Alf hid behind a hay bale. **"Time to load the sleigh,"** said Santa, cheerily.

Soon, Santa's sleigh was packed with presents and ready for take-off. But as the elves went to push the barn doors open, they realised something was wrong.

The doors are frozen shut! We need to break them down!

yelled the chief elf.

Alf jumped out of his hiding place. **"I can help!"** he beamed.
After all, he was good at breaking things.

Just then, poor Alf tripped over a box of sleigh bells. The noise
sent the reindeers crashing antlers-first through the barn doors.

Alf gulped, he was sure he was for it now. But Santa was chuckling.

The chief elf gave Alf a pat on the back.
"It seems you've saved Christmas!" he said with a cheer.

No More Mince Pies

It was Christmas Eve in Katie and Harry's house and excitement filled the air. They wanted to make sure everything was perfect for Santa's arrival, so they set to work hanging their stockings on the mantelpiece and decorating the tree.

Their **cheeky** puppy Scruff wanted to help, too.
When Katie placed a sparkling bauble on the tree...

... Scruff nudged it and sent it
spinning across the floor!

When Harry cleared logs
from the fireplace...

... Scruff left sooty paw prints
across the carpet!

"The tree is nearly ready!" cried Katie.
"Let's go and get Santa's mince pie and hot chocolate ready."

Harry and Katie left a warm mince pie and mug of hot chocolate in
the kitchen, then went to finish off the decorations in the living room.

Suddenly, they heard a loud...

Crash!

Harry and Katie **rushed** into the kitchen to find...

... Scruff surrounded by mince pie crumbs and a broken plate.

"That was the last mince pie and there's no hot chocolate left either. Now all we have to give Santa is a cup of tea and some toast!" sniffed Katie.

That night, Katie and Harry went to bed feeling very **glum** indeed.

As the children slept, Santa landed on the roof of their house.

"Oh, Dasher! If I see another mince pie or mug of hot chocolate, I don't know what I'll do," said Santa. "I've already eaten 21,567 mince pies this evening!"

In the living room, Santa saw the
toast and cup of tea. He was **delighted!**
"Just what I fancied," he chuckled.
And with that, he left a little note
and carried on his way.

The next morning, Katie, Harry and Scruff bounded into the living room. **"Wow!"** cried Harry, holding up Santa's note. **"Look at this!"**

It read, 'Same again next year, please!'

They were delighted, it had been a **perfect** Christmas Eve after all.

Christmas Fairy

It was time to decorate the tree and Eva couldn't wait to put up all the decorations. Dad had been up in the attic and soon the hallway was filled with tinsel, baubles and ornaments.

When the Christmas tree was nearly finished, Eva grabbed the box that contained the most special tree decoration of all, the Christmas fairy.

But as she opened the lid, she discovered that one of the fairy's wings was broken.

"Don't worry," said Mum.
"Let's dash to the shops to see
if we can buy a new fairy."

But Eva really didn't want a
new fairy. Her fairy was the most
beautiful Christmas fairy, ever.

If we must,

said Eva, sighing sadly.

When Eva and her mum arrived at the shop, it was filled with fairies of all different shapes and sizes, but none of them were quite right. Their dresses weren't sparkly enough and their smiles weren't quite as bright as Eva's old fairy.

"I have an idea!" said Mum, enthusiastically. "All we need is a little bit of magic, and a trip to the craft shop."
Eva was a bit confused, but she followed her mum.

Back home, Mum and Eva laid the broken fairy on the kitchen table.

There were pots of glue,
scraps of material and glitter.
Together they made a new wing
for the fairy and even added extra
sparkle to her old dress.

When they had finished, Eva proudly held the fairy up high. Her pretty new wings were made of **glittering** material and they sparkled in the glow of the fairy lights.

Eva had to admit, she looked even better than last year.

"Now we just have to place
her at the top of the tree," said Dad.

Eva giggled. "She's perfect!" she said.

The Runaway Reindeer

It was Christmas Eve. Jack was hanging up his old Christmas stocking when his big brother Tom bounded into their room.

"Where's your stocking?" asked Jack. "Santa won't know where to put your presents if you don't hang one up."

Tom laughed. "You don't still believe in Santa do you?" he said. "Come on, let's get some sleep."

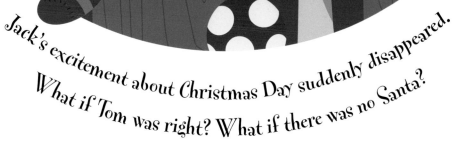

Jack's excitement about Christmas Day suddenly disappeared. What if Tom was right? What if there was no Santa?

Jack lay awake in bed for
a long time, thinking.

Suddenly, he heard a **clattering**
noise and the **tinkling** of bells.

He jumped out of bed and peeked out of his curtains.
There, in his back garden, was a **real** reindeer!

"**Psst!**" said Jack, waking Tom up.
"**There's a reindeer in our back garden.**"

Huh? Don't be silly, Jack,

yawned Tom.

But Jack wasn't being silly and he was going to prove it.
He crept downstairs, taking his sleepy big brother with him.

Jack opened the back door. Sure enough,
there was the reindeer, munching on a holly bush.

We'd better try
and catch him!

said Tom,
looking amazed.

But as the boys got closer, the reindeer began to dart around...

... this way

... and that.

The reindeer had a different plan in mind.
He was having far too much fun to be
caught by Jack and Tom. Each time
they made a grab for him...

... the boys went **slipping** and **sliding** in the snow.

The reindeer **trampled** Mum's vegetable patch and knocked over Dad's plant pots, shaking his bells as he pranced. But Jack had an idea.

Quick, go and get some carrots!

said Jack, as Tom dashed to the kitchen.

Jack and Tom coaxed the reindeer into a corner of the garden and stroked his nose. **"That was fun,"** giggled Tom.

"What should we do?" replied Jack. "Santa will be missing him." Tom smiled kindly. "I've told you, there's no such thing as.."

... Just then, the garden gate swung open
and in walked **Santa!**

Santa! cried Jack, as he
gave Santa a big hug.

Tom rubbed his eyes in **amazement.**
"Ho, ho, ho! Thank you, boys," boomed Santa
"You've found my lost reindeer!"

Soon, Santa and his reindeer were back in the air. **"Here's an extra something for you both!"** said Santa, dropping two gifts from his sleigh.

Tom and Jack **tore** off the wrapping to reveal a brand-new Christmas stocking each.

The next morning, Tom couldn't believe his eyes as he opened his pile of presents. **"It's the football boots I wanted,"** he said. **"How did Santa know?"**

Don't you get it by now? grinned Jack

The real Santa always knows...